The Extra-special Helper
published in 2010 by
Hardie Grant Egmont
Ground floor, Building 1, 658 Church Street
Richmond, Victoria 3121, Australia
www.hardiegrantegmont.com.au

A CiP record for this title is available from the National Library of Australia

Text copyright © 2010 Sally Rippin
Illustration copyright © 2010 Aki Fukuoka
Logo and design copyright © 2010 Hardie Grant Egmont

Design and typeset by Stephanie Spartels

Printed in China by Everbest Printing

The
Extra-special
Helper

By Sally Rippin

Illustrated by Aki Fukuoka

hardie grant EGMONT

Chapter One

Billie B Brown has one
sun hat, one water bottle
and fourteen clipboards.
Do you want to know
what the B in Billie
B Brown stands for?

Bossy.

Billie B Brown can
sometimes be just a teensy
bit bossy. Like today,
for example. Billie and
her class are going on an
excursion. They are going
to the zoo.

Do you know why Billie
is carrying so many
clipboards?

Fourteen clipboards

Sun hat

Water bottle

Ms Walton has asked
Billie to be her
extra-special helper.

Billie is helping
Ms Walton carry all
the clipboards for their
excursion. Usually Ella
and Tracey get to be
Ms Walton's helpers,
but today Ms Walton
has chosen Billie.

Billie feels very **proud**.
She gets to sit next to
Ms Walton on the bus.

'You will have to help
me make sure nobody
gets lost today, Billie,'
Ms Walton says. 'It's a

very important job.'

'Of course,' says Billie.

'OK, now, not so much
noise, please!' Ms Walton
calls out to the boys at
the back of the bus.

Billie turns around to look.

The boys at the back are

making a lot of **noise**.

Billie waves to Jack.

Jack is Billie's best friend.

They have been

best friends since they

were babies.

Usually Billie and Jack

sit together.

But today Billie is being
Ms Walton's extra-special
helper, so Jack is sitting
with the other boys at
the back of the bus.

The boys are laughing and
Sam is singing a loud song.

'Billie,' Ms Walton says,
'can you please go and
ask the boys to keep it
down a bit?'

Billie walks to the back
of the bus.

'You boys are making
too much noise!' she says.

'Who says?' asks Sam.

'Yeah, who says?' asks
Benny.

Benny is Sam's
best friend.

'Ms Walton,'
says Billie.
'She told me to
tell you to keep it down.'

Benny looks at Jack.
Sam looks at Jack.

Jack shrugs. 'Sorry, Billie,' he says. 'We'll try to be quieter.'

'Good!' says Billie, and she marches back to the front of the bus.

'Thank you, Billie,' Ms Walton says.

Billie beams. She likes being an extra-special helper.

Chapter Two

When they get to the zoo, Ms Walton tells the class to form two lines. One line is in front of Ms Walton, and the other line is in front of Billie.

Ms Walton and Billie
hand out the clipboards.

'Now, hold on to
your clipboards, please,'
says Ms Walton. 'I want
them all back at the end
of the day.'

'Don't lose the
clipboards,' Billie says,
handing them out to
Benny, Sam and Jack.

Jack frowns. 'I won't!'
he says.

'I'm just saying, that's all,'
says Billie, walking down
the line.

'Now, everyone stay together,' Ms Walton says. 'I don't want to lose anyone, OK?'

'**OK**!' everyone in Billie's class shouts.

They are all very **excited**. A day at the zoo is much more fun than school!

'Great!' says Ms Walton.

'First we are going to look at the reptiles.

I want you to put the animals you see today into two groups: warm-blooded and cold-blooded, OK?'

Benny puts up his hand. 'What's warm-blooded and cold-blooded?'

16

Ms Walton sighs. 'Benny, we have been learning about this all term!'

'Don't worry, Ms Walton,' Billie says. 'I'll help Benny.'

Benny frowns. 'No, thanks,' he says. 'You are already helping Ms Walton. Jack can help me.'

'Sure!' says Jack.

Jack swings his arm over Benny's shoulder. 'It's easy. Look.'

Billie watches Benny and Jack talking together. She feels a teensy bit **jealous**.

Usually Jack is her
partner in class. But then
Ms Walton asks Billie
to help her hand out
pencils and Billie feels
important again.

'Billie, I need you to
walk at the end of the
line to make sure no-one
gets left behind,' says
Ms Walton.

Billie scrunches up her forehead. She doesn't want to walk at the end of the line. She wants to walk in the middle of the line with Jack. Or up the front with Ms Walton.

But Ms Walton has asked Billie to be her extra-special helper today, so Billie nods.

'Um, OK,' says Billie.

'Thank you,' says
Ms Walton. 'It's very
important no-one
gets lost. The zoo is a
very big place!'

Chapter Three

The class walk in two lines to the reptile house. Billie walks at the end of the two lines to make sure nobody gets lost. She has a very important job to do!

They look at the lizards
and tortoises and
crocodiles. Billie knows
that these animals are all
cold-blooded. They have
studied this in class.
She writes them down
on her list.

Next, they go to
look at the monkeys.
The monkeys are Billie's
favourite. Billie especially
loves the baby chimpanzees.
They are so cheeky!
Billie puts monkeys
under the warm-blooded
heading. Too easy!

Billie looks up from
her clipboard.

Sam, Benny and Jack are pulling silly faces at the monkeys. Billie thinks they look very funny. They look like monkeys themselves! She giggles.

But then Ms Walton looks over. 'Come on, boys!' she calls. 'You're holding up the line!'

Billie marches over to the boys. She had almost forgotten her important job. She has to make sure no-one gets left behind!

'Hurry up!' she says.

'Come on! Everyone's
waiting!'

'You are very bossy today,
Billie!' says Jack.

Billie looks at Jack.
He is not making a silly
monkey face anymore.
He is not even making
a happy Jack face.

He is making a very
cross face. And he is
making that cross face
at Billie!

Billie feels all **jumbled up**
inside. She wants Jack to
be happy with her.

Jack is her best friend.

But she wants Ms Walton
to be happy with her, too.
She is Ms Walton's
extra-special helper.
Billie doesn't want to let
her down.

Billie frowns. 'I'm not
bossy. I just have to make
sure no-one gets lost!'
she says.

She walks behind
the boys to the back of
the line. If Jack is **cross**
with her then she is
cross with him, too!

The class walks out of
the monkey area and
along the path to their
next stop. They look at
the lions and tigers and
the long-necked giraffes.

Then they walk through
the steamy butterfly room.

Billie writes down all
the animals on her sheet
of paper. She knows all
the answers.

Chapter Four

Soon they come to the sea creatures. They go into a dark tunnel under the water.

Billie stands in front of the glass and watches the dolphins.

They duck and weave
and **chatter**. Billie thinks
they are wonderful.

A baby dolphin swims
next to his mother,
bobbing his head up
and down. Billie waves and
the baby dolphin opens
his mouth into a big smile.

Hmmm, Billie wonders.

Are dolphins warm-blooded or cold-blooded?

Billie can't remember.

Do baby dolphins come out of eggs?

She isn't sure.

Billie has an idea.

She will ask Jack for help.

Every time Billie is
stuck on a question
in class, Jack helps her.
If Jack gets stuck, Billie
helps him. That's what
best friends do.

Billie looks around for Jack.
But Jack is nowhere
to be seen. In fact, the
whole class has gone!
Billie has been left behind!

Billie runs out of
the tunnel. She looks
to the left. Nobody!
She looks to the right.
Nobody! Billie is lost!
She feels like she is going
to cry.

Suddenly, from around
the corner, a face appears.
The face has freckles
and a big goofy smile.
Do you know who it is?

That's right, it's Jack!
He has come back
for Billie. She has never
been so happy to see him.

'Come on, Billie,' he jokes.

'You're holding everyone up!'

Billie blushes. 'Sorry for being so bossy before,' she says. 'Thanks for coming back.'

'That's OK,' says Jack, holding Billie's hand. 'I know you were just trying to help Ms Walton.'

'I was so worried about everyone else getting lost that I got lost myself!' says Billie.

'Lucky I noticed that you were gone,' says Jack.

Billie feels lucky to
have such a good friend.
Then she has an idea.
'Hey, will you walk at
the back with me?'

'Sure,' says Jack, smiling.
Then suddenly, he
frowns. 'Oh no!' he says.

'What?' asks Billie.
She is **worried** he may
have changed his mind.

Maybe he doesn't want to walk with her anymore?

'Your clipboard! Where is it?' Jack says.

'Oh, I must have left it near the dolphins!' Billie gasps. 'I am not a very good helper today, am I?' she says. 'I think I need my own extra-special helper!'

Jack laughs. 'Come on. Let's go and get your clipboard before we are *both* lost!' he says.

'You are very bossy today, Jack,' says Billie. But she is smiling.

They both run back into the tunnel to find the clipboard.

Then they run as fast as they can to join the end of the line again.

And do you know what? They are so fast that nobody even notices they were gone!